We Both   ite parents and childrer   ns reading aloud. This   oped with reading edu   e complex text and sto   ouraged to read the righ   l storyline, specifically

Reading   arents can share with   elopment. However, *We*   ws parents to share the r   d effective because it co   (the parent reads) and "(er reading development   enriching experience f

You ma   ourself the first time, th   eading. In some books,   ced in the parent's text   and even discussing, t   them and help to build   ng parent" icon ◌ prec   precedes the child's te

We enco   you read the book togetuer. If your child is having difficulty, you might want to mention a few things to help them. "Sounding out" is good, but it will not work with all words. Children can pick up clues about the words they are reading from the story, the context of the sentence, or even the pic-tures. Some stories have rhyming patterns that might help. It might also help them to touch the words with their finger as they read, to better connect the voice sound and the printed word.

Sharing the *We Both Read* books together will engage you and your child in an interactive adventure in reading! It is a fun and easy way to encourage and help your child to read—and a wonderful way to start them off on a lifetime of reading enjoyment!

We Both Read: A Pony Named Peanut

We Both Read® is a trademark of Treasure Bay, Inc.

Published by Treasure Bay, Inc.
40 Sir Francis Drake Boulevard
San Anselmo, CA 94960 USA

PRINTED IN SINGAPORE

Library of Congress Catalog Card Number: 2007932566

Hardcover ISBN-10: 1-60115-015-6
Hardcover ISBN-13: 978-1-60115-015-8
Paperback ISBN-10: 1-60115-016-4
Paperback ISBN-13: 978-1-60115-016-5

We Both Read® Books
Patent No. 5,957,693

Visit us online at:
www.webothread.com

WE BOTH READ ®

A Pony Named Peanut

By Sindy McKay

Illustrated by Meredith Johnson

FRIDAY, *June 13th*

This summer was going to be totally fantastic!

It WAS going to be fantastic. Now it's going to totally stink.

I ALWAYS spend the summer with my Aunt Rachel in the city, where there are a million stores and you can go shopping every day if you want to. But my mom told me, "Jessica, your Aunt Rachel is going to Europe this year, so you get to spend the summer in the **country** instead!"

I hate the **country**. At least, I think I hate the **country**. I've never been to the **country**, but it sure sounds boring.

I'm spending the summer with my Uncle Bill and Aunt Molly in a place called Texas. I've only met them once before, when I was about four years old. That was a whole four years ago! I don't even remember what they look like.

Mom thinks it's time I get to know them better. That's why she's sending me to spend a month with them. That's four whole weeks!

I feel like I'm going to jail.

🔄 *SATURDAY, June 14th*

The country is weird. Not weird in a bad way—just *weird*.

My Aunt and Uncle live in a big house with land all around it. You can't even see the house next door. They have a long driveway you have to drive up to get to their house, and on the way you see a bunch of horses and goats.

Near the house there's a barn. Outside of the barn are chickens. Inside of the barn are more horses.

The horses are really big! Aunt Molly says I can ride one if I want to.

I do not want to. Ever.

Uncle Bill told me that almost all of the animals here came from the local animal **shelter**. I asked if that was the same as the dog pound and he said yes, but there are more than just dogs there. The **shelter** rescues all kinds of animals.

Uncle Bill is going to the **shelter** on Monday. He wants to look at a pony they have.

He asked me if I wanted to go with him. I asked him if the **shelter** was in a shopping mall. He said, "No." So I said, "No, thank you."

🐾 MONDAY, *June 16th*

    Uncle Bill came home today with that pony from the shelter.

    I thought a pony was a little tiny horse, but this pony is definitely not little. She's almost as big as a regular horse! Aunt Molly thinks she's totally the perfect size for me to ride.

    I think Aunt Molly is totally wrong.

Aunt Molly asked me if I wanted to name the new pony. I thought King Kong would be a good name. Aunt Molly thought something like Tiny might be better. We decided on Peanut.

She is definitely the biggest Peanut I've ever seen.

Uncle Bill asked me to give Peanut a carrot. I didn't really want to, so I told him, "Maybe **tomorrow**." He just smiled and told me to lay the carrot across the palm of my hand and let Peanut do the rest.

Her breath was hot and her soft lips tickled my hand when she took the carrot in her mouth.

It felt kind of creepy—but also kind of cool!

I asked Uncle Bill if I could give her another one. He said one was enough for today. I could give her another one **tomorrow**.

🐴 *TUESDAY, June 17th*

Today I woke up early and went to the barn to give Peanut her carrot. When I turned to walk away, she nudged me in the back with her nose and knocked me right down on my rear end!

I heard someone **laughing** and looked up to see Max. He's a boy who comes here every morning to help with the chores.

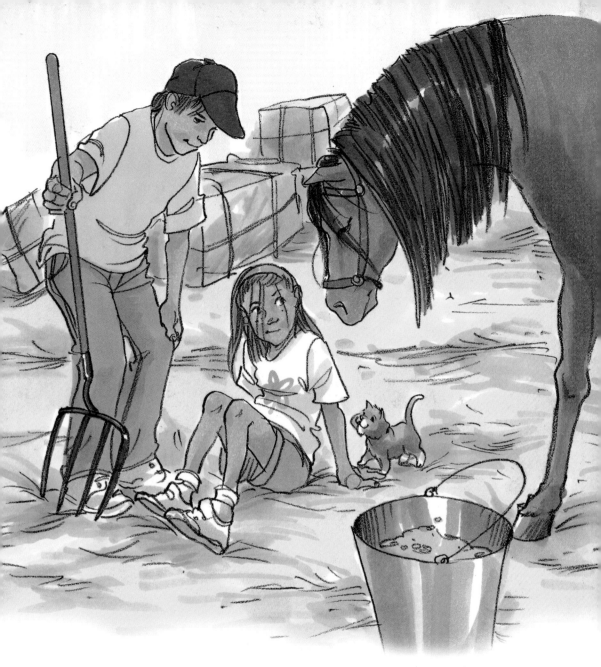

Max told me that Peanut didn't mean to knock me over. She was just looking for another carrot. Peanut nodded her head up and down. Max said she was **laughing** at me too.

I think she was saying she was sorry.

Max asked me to help him with the chores. There's nothing else to do around here, so I said okay.

As we worked, Max told me about Peanut. She used to walk around in a circle all day, giving kids a pony ride. That's all she did for nine years. Now that she has more freedom, she's afraid to try new things. She won't even go out in the field to graze on the grass.

I told Max I'd never been on a pony ride. I'd never been on a pony at all. He said, "There's a first time for everything. You can ride Peanut!"

I said, "No way." Then he said I was afraid to try new things too. Just like Peanut.

So I stuck out my tongue at him.

☺WEDNESDAY, *June 18th*

Aunt Molly was supposed to take me to the mall today, but something came up, so she'll take me tomorrow instead. That's okay, because when I went to the barn, Max asked me to help him **groom** Peanut!

Max used a curry comb to bring up all the dirt on Peanut's coat. Then I brushed off the dirt with something called a dandy brush.

   After that, I brushed Peanut all over with a soft brush.
Max gave me a special comb to **groom** her mane and her
"pony tail." Peanut tried to **groom** MY ponytail too!

Tonight at dinner, I told Uncle Bill all about grooming Peanut today. He told me that tomorrow someone was coming to look at the feet of all the horses. Taking care of their feet is very important and a special person called a *farrier* comes every six weeks to look at them.

I asked Uncle Bill if I could watch the **farrier**. Aunt Molly reminded me that we were going shopping tomorrow. I asked if maybe we could go shopping another day. Aunt Molly smiled and said that would be just fine.

The stuff that the farrier does is so cool! A horse's **hooves** grow like fingernails, so he uses a *rasp*—this thing that looks like a giant emery board—to file them down. He did a bunch of other stuff, then asked if I wanted to try using a *hoof pick*. I said I didn't know how and he said he'd show me. I said, "Great!" But I didn't really mean it.

The farrier showed me how to get Peanut to pick up her feet. He showed me how to use the hoof pick to clean stuff out from under her **hooves**. Then he said, "Now YOU try it."

I didn't want to, but Max was watching. So I had to try.

I did what the farrier had showed me, but Peanut wouldn't pick up her foot. He suggested I take a deep **breath** and try again. But Peanut STILL wouldn't pick up her foot. I was so **frustrated** that I almost gave up! Then the farrier asked if I had ridden Peanut yet, and Max told him that I don't like to try new things.

That made me kind of mad.

The farrier could see that I was mad. He told me that horses can feel when we are mad or **frustrated**. They don't like it. He said I should try to be calm. So I took another deep **breath** and tried again. Peanut picked up her foot!

I stuck my tongue out at Max again.

🐾 *WEDNESDAY, June 25th*

    Oh, I just love Peanut! I took care of her this whole week. I fed her and I watered her and I groomed her and I cleaned out her hooves. Then yesterday, Max let me hold the *lunge line* when he took her out for exercise in the riding ring. I held the line, while Max called out **directions**. He told me to guide her around in a circle.

Then Max told me to turn her in the other **direction**.
At first she didn't want to. She only went in one **direction**
when she gave pony rides. Max said to take our time.
It was hard for Peanut, but she finally did it. Yesterday
was a great day!

This morning, Aunt Molly finally took me shopping at the local mall. I bought myself a really cool pair of red cowboy boots. I couldn't wait to get home so I could take Peanut out and **lunge** her around the riding ring in my new boots. Max told me boots are for riding, not for lunging.

Peanut went in both directions on the **lunge** line—no problem! Uncle Bill thinks she is coming along nicely. He thinks it's time someone rode her. He thinks it should be me.

I think he's wrong.

SATURDAY, *July 5th*

    Uncle Bill told me it was much better for Peanut to be ridden than to just be exercised on a lunge line. "**Jessica**," he kept saying, "you want to do what's best for Peanut, don't you?"

    So I finally agreed to try it.

    At first I was really scared. Then Max said, *"Little kids* used to ride this horse. If *they* can do it, *you* can do it!" I stuck out my tongue at him again as he helped me in the saddle.

   All of a sudden there I was—on top of Peanut.
Can you believe it?? Me! **Jessica** Ames! Riding a
horse! It was amazing!!

"Great job, **Jessica**," cheered Uncle Bill.

Max grinned at me and said, "Your new red boots
look really good up there."

It's so cool to be sitting on Peanut's back. Max taught me how to give her a gentle kick with my heels and make a clucking noise to get her walking.

The first two days we just walked around the ring. Then Max showed me how to make her trot. I go **bouncing** all over the place when Peanut trots! (But Max is helping me work on that.)

Today I got Peanut to **canter**.

A canter is faster than a trot and you hardly **bounce** at all. I love to **canter**. I love going fast. I love not **bouncing**. I love everything about this horse!

◯ *WEDNESDAY, July 9th*

Yesterday Max taught me how to put the saddle and bridle on Peanut and now I can do it all by myself. It is just so totally cool!!!

We've been riding in the ring all week, but today Aunt Molly and Uncle Bill saddled up their own horses for a trail ride. They said it was time for Peanut to face her fears. It was time for her to go out of the riding ring.

Uncle Bill said that I was the best person to take her out. I could help her do something new. After all, she had helped ME do something new. She had helped me take my first pony ride.

I knew that if I was nervous, Peanut would be nervous too, so I climbed on board and **urged** her forward confidently. She happily did just what I asked until we reached the gate—then she stopped so suddenly that I almost fell off!

I leaned down and whispered to her, "It's okay, Peanut. It's good to try something new. In fact, it's wonderful."

I **urged** her forward again. She tossed her head and walked out of the ring. Max shouted, "It's about time! For BOTH of you!" I laughed—and stuck my tongue out at him.

We rode the trails around my Uncle's house all morning. It was the most fun I've ever had in my whole entire life!

I can't believe a whole month has gone by and I have to go home tomorrow. I'm going to miss Peanut so much! And, of course, Uncle Bill and Aunt Molly and Max too.

Uncle Bill told me I had done a great thing. I had helped Peanut overcome her fear and she would remember that when I came back next year.

 I was so glad he said that part about me coming back. I can't wait until next summer!

Now I really love the country. And it's all because of a pony named Peanut.

When looking for a new pet, many of us go to our local animal shelter. Often these shelters are run by the ASPCA— the American Society for the Prevention of Cruelty to Animals. The ASPCA is an organization that is working hard to make the world a safe place for all animals. Their goal is to make sure that all animals are treated with respect and kindness.

To find out more about the ASPCA, ask your parents about visiting their website at www.aspca.org — or the ASPCA's special site just for kids at www.animaland.org !

The next time you are looking for a new pet, visit your local animal shelter. You'll be happy you did!

Glossary of horse equipment

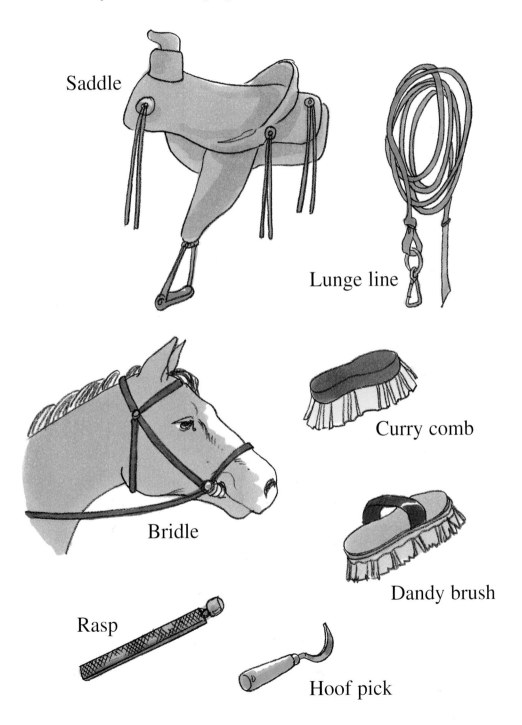

Saddle

Lunge line

Curry comb

Bridle

Dandy brush

Rasp

Hoof pick

If you liked **A Pony Named Peanut**, here is another
We Both Read® Book you are sure to enjoy!

Ben and Becky finally convince their parents to let
them have a pet. Becky wants to get a kitten, but Ben
wants to get a snake. They go with their father to pick
out a pet and cause hilarious excitement when they
accidentally let the pet store's snake loose in the mall!